MW00889650

Coleman and Vaughn,

You guys are the inspiration for this book.

Our time working together has been priceless.

I love you,

Grampa

Dragon Adventure

A Sir Coleman and Sir Vaughn Adventure

By Kevin Wixom

One day, Vaughn and Coleman were building block castles.

"I wish we could play in real castles," Vaughn said.

"We could fight dragons and wear armor and ride big war horses."

"Oh no. Vaughn, what is happening?"

Suddenly, the boys were outside.

"Vaughn, you're a knight!"

"You too, Coleman."

"Look, it's Katie and Bennie,"
Vaughn said. "They came too."

"We shall call them Kathryn and
Benedict and they shall be our
valiant steeds."

"Why are you talking so weird,"
Coleman said.

The boys decided to explore this new world. They climbed onto Kathryn and Benedict and started riding.

Soon they saw a castle.

"Look, yon castle beckons," Vaughn said.

"What?" Coleman said. "Stop talking like that. Come on, let's go meet those people."

They didn't see the dragon hiding in the bushes.

Suddenly, the dragon jumped into the air and flew over the boys.

They pulled out their swords, ready for anything.

"Hello, Sir Knights.
Thank you for coming
to our world. We need
your help to vanquish
an evil upon our
lands.
Will you help us?" said
the dragon.

"We shall endeavour to assist you in your just cause," said Vaughn.

"Woa, what? What endeavour?" Coleman said.

"Follow me, brave knights. I shall lead you to glory," said Karl.

"Lead on, noble dragon," Vaughn said.

"Wait, where are we going?" Coleman asked.

"Pay no attention to that knight. He will not help us with our quest.

We must hurry," Karl said. "We are going into the dark forest."

The boys followed Karl into
the dark forest.

With a BANG, a wizard appeared in front of them.

"Who trespasses into my forest?" the wizard demanded.

"Are you friend or enemy?"

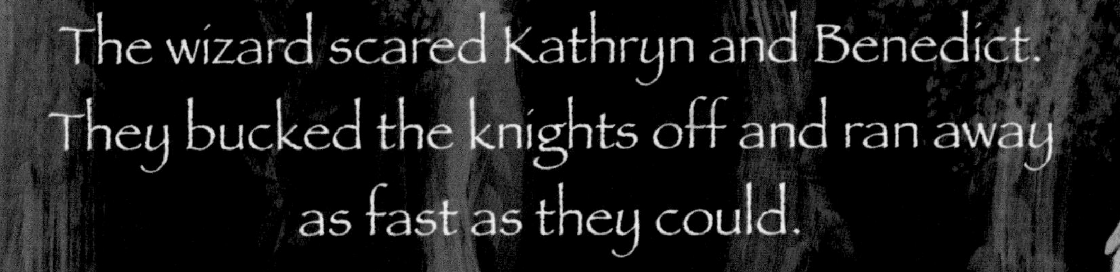

The wizard scared Kathryn and Benedict.
They bucked the knights off and ran away
as fast as they could.

"It is I, Karl. I brought you knights."

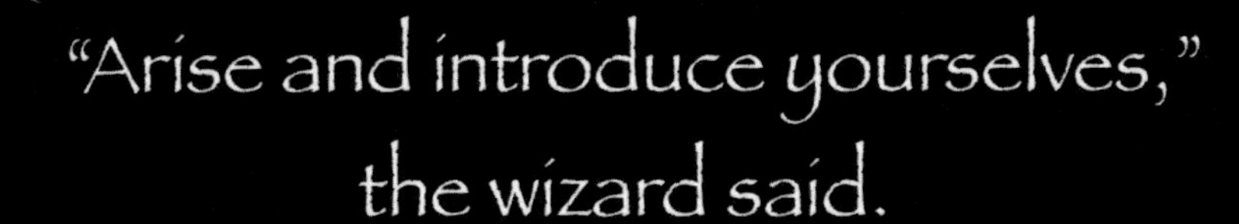

"Arise and introduce yourselves,"
the wizard said.
Instead, the boys jumped up and
grabbed their swords.

The wizard
blasted their
swords into the
air.

"Do not raise your swords to me, young knights. I wish you to join me in a quest."

He waived his wand and vines grabbed the boys and hung them upside down.

"I release you, but if you misbehave I will turn you into frogs."

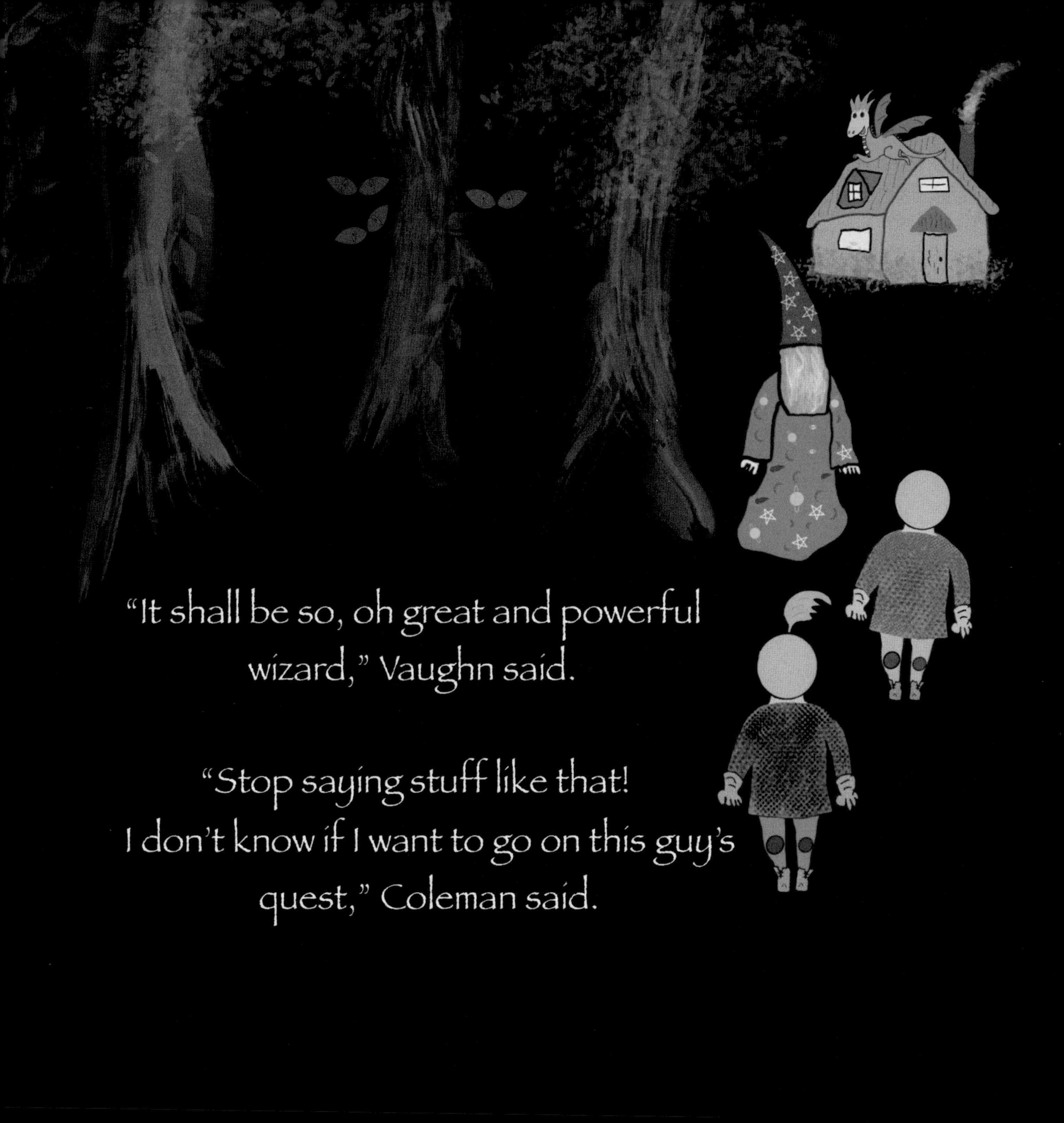

"It shall be so, oh great and powerful wizard," Vaughn said.

"Stop saying stuff like that! I don't know if I want to go on this guy's quest," Coleman said.

"I am Gooboogooboo and this is my pet pterodactyl, Wingie. My friends call me Goob."

"I am Vaughn and this is Coleman, said Vaughn."

"Welcome, Sir Coleman and Sir Vaughn. Please, sit."

Goob poured tea and explained his plan.
"Kackles the witch is the evil in this forest. I can only catch her if she doesn't see me. To do that, I need two decoys."

"You want us to get the attention of an evil witch?" Coleman asked.

"Yes," Goob said. "I do."

Goob pulled out his wand and, POOF,
the tea was gone and the boys had
their shields and swords.
"Now, go find the witch and keep her
busy while I sneak up on her," Goob
commanded. "Good luck."

The boys snuck through the forest and soon found Kackles. She saw them.

"Ahhhh, what have we here? Two young knights. Just what I need to finish my magic potion. Which of you would like to take a hot bath in my cauldron?"

"Coleman, run! She saw us coming!" They turned and ran away from Kackles as fast as they could.

"She's cursing us. Keep your shield up!" Vaughn yelled.

"Run little knights. You can't hide from me. I'll catch you and put you in my cauldron," Kackles cackled.

Kackles chased them all the way
out of the forest.
As they turned to fight, Wingie
caught up and pecked Kackles
on the head.

Kackles spun in the air and blasted Wingie with her wand. “That will teach you to peck me,” she said.

"Now, my little knights. I'm going to turn you into frogs and cook you in my cauldron."

Vaughn rushed at Kackles and hit her broom with his sword.

Coleman attacked too. "You killed Wingie!"

Kackles blasted their swords and shields away and knocked them to the ground.

"Now my little knights, you're coming with me. Into my cauldron you go. Ha ha ha ha."

Just in time, Goob appeared and cast a spell on the witch.
"Get into my magic jar, witch!"
The boys fell to the ground and ran to Wingie. He was alive!

"We did it! Kackles is trapped in this jar. How can we ever repay you?" said Goob.

"We would like to go home now. Can you send us home?" asked Coleman.

"If that is what you wish, I can send you home right now," said Goob.

"Brave and honorable knights, prepare to be transported. Close your eyes.

One, two and zoooom!"

Suddenly, the boys were back home.

"Was that a dream?" Coleman said.

"Maybe," Vaughn said, "but I don't think so."

"Where are Bennie
and Katie,"
Coleman asked.
Karl waved a wing
and winked.

Karl was gone and Katie and Bennie were back.

The boys sighed and began work on their castles again.

Crack!

"What was that noise," Vaughn asked.

"Woo hoo!!"
Goob had given them a present after all.

The
End

Made in the USA
Middletown, DE
11 November 2022